Krieg

Naomi Lee Reid

Published by Naomi Reid, 2023.

This is a work of fiction. Similarities to real people, places, or events are entirely coincidental.

KRIEG

First edition. November 30, 2023.

Copyright © 2023 Naomi Lee Reid.

ISBN: 979-8223281146

Written by Naomi Lee Reid.

Table of Contents

This book is for all those who fought in the *Krieg*, and for everyone whose soldier didn't make it back.

CHAPTER ONE

WE WERE HERDED LIKE animals into the military camp.

They looked at us like we were meant to be stared at. They looked at our teeth, our hair, our arms and legs; our whole bodies, it seemed. We were criticized for how skinny or heavy we were. They ran their hands over our arms, inspecting our forearms and biceps to see if we had muscles to spare. Muscles that would get us a good position in the *Krieg*. The war. I was one of the several to be decided as a soldier. Not because I had muscles, which I hardly did, decidedly. It was because I could be of use. That is, to die for Germany without Hitler himself kicking the bucket. Me and seventeen others from that truck. All I could think of was Sharon... and my three children. Where were they? Were they alright?

We were taken to these rooms I will never forget. People were forced to have most of their hair shaved away, into these crewcuts. They were being assigned uniforms—dark gray green, with a *Swastika* on the arm. I was German. I didn't salute their flag.

We were being drafted for the German Army, 1939. World War II was starting. Not a lot knew it at the beginning. I knew. I could feel the taste of it—bitter and full of blood, with hate brewing behind it. Of course, Adolf Hitler was behind it all. He started that *Krieg*. And I would never forget those years I was forced to see SS officers, and the Nazis, and all the Jews they—we—took captive.

Even after the *Krieg* I still feel like I had never gotten stronger in it. The things I had seen... and so many people's blood was on my hands. But I was doing this from force. I was not doing this for my country because I wanted to. I was doing it because I was German, and Germans, as we were told while we lined up against the walls in the uniforms, were born and bred to deliver one thing in 1939: death.

"RICHTEN SIE AUF! BEEILEN SIE SICH! JETZT!" one of the commanders screamed at us. We were pushed in single-file lines, up and down the hall. I counted eighteen rows, made up of around twenty to thirty people in each.

The commander, with his dark mustache and white-blonde hair and blue eyes, walked slowly down each row, shouting at the top of his lungs:

"SIND SIE HIER, UM HITLER ZU DIENEN. DU BIST HIER, UM DEN JUDEN DAS LEBEN ZU NEHMEN. WIR WERDEN REGIEREN. DIE JUDEN WERDEN UNTER UNSEREN STIEFELN STERBEN WIR WERDEN REGIEREN!"

You are here to serve Hitler. You are here to take the lives of the Jews. We will rule. We will rule.

The words rang in my head, in the hall. I wanted to shut them out, but I couldn't. The only thing I could think of was Sharon, Nikita, Tevis, and Heinrich. And that my own people were going out with rifles over their shoulders to kill those of my wife's heritage. Then the commander shouted, *"HEIL HITLER,"* and the hall rang with the words.

"Heil Hitler," they all said, their voices running together and making one booming voice. Most were glad to *heil.* It made me feel sick.

"Heil Hitler," I said with them, barley whispering, my throat too tight and dry to say what would now be the name of who I served. *Sie sind hier, um Hitler zu dienen.* You are here to serve Hitler.

I didn't hear the rest of what the commander said. That was my mistake. And it resulted in the commander coming to me, and saying in his voice that was loud and brutal, *"Was ist Ihr name?* What is your name?"

I couldn't speak. I was more horrified than I was a year later in that ravine.

"What is your name?" the commander repeated. This time he took his gun, using the end of it to tip my head back. The metal was cold. I felt my hands shaking.

"Schneider," I said, my voice a croak. The commander narrowed his blue eyes and stared into mine, a dull blue-gray color and what must have held horror behind them. Everyone watched. The commander's stare bored into me until the end of his gun lowered. My breath caught. He straightened, bringing himself to be higher and more menacing. He shouted at those looking our way, *"Schauen Sie nach vorne. Beruhigt."*

Everyone looked ahead, their arms behind their backs. I was hissed at to do the same, and I did. I felt like my breath would leave me completely. I thought that the blood flow to my head was slowing, making me feel cold and dizzy. I just stared ahead. I was filled with worry.

Because I wasn't a true German. I was of German blood, *ja,* I had been born in Berlin, I had been raised to hate Jews and to serve the German flag. The flag of Germany, maybe, but not the Swastika, the flag with the crooked Arian cross. And those who didn't support Hitler, or sported the Swastika, paid the price. They paid dearly.

CHAPTER TWO

WE WERE TRAINING FROM 4:00 in the morning to 12:00 at night. It was brutal training—I thought it was nearly unbearable. After the first day I threw up for nearly thirty minutes, on and off. But I knew I couldn't *not* do it. Because I had to. It did not matter that I had a right to refuse this—any other time I did have the right to say so. Not here. Here I was one of the hundreds who were drafted mercilessly.

That night in the bunks I had the most realistic, most horrifying dream I had ever had. It was where I was being taken by men in uniforms. They were dragging me, beat and bleeding, to the rocky edge of a ravine. They held me still for a fraction of a moment, and then pushed me, letting go of the back of my neck and throwing me off the side. I fell and hit the millions of small and large rocks, falling down the side of the ravine, every bit of rock cutting into my skin, until I landed hard on the bottom. I didn't move. And I could see the black shapes of the men in uniforms in front of the glaring sun, which burned my eyes, until they closed, and I couldn't see anything anymore.

Then I had been awoken by the sound of Lieutenant Raus slamming the door to the room open and barking for all ten of us to get up. I wasted no time doing so. It might be a military camp, but they had no problem putting a bullet through our chests if they wanted. "*Steh auf!*" he said, his voice unpleasant this early in the morning. "Get up! We're burning daylight!"

We most certainly weren't. Not at four in the morning. I didn't say so.

"*Steh auf! Schnell!*" When one of us would pass him, he would hit us hard on the back. When he did so to me I nearly staggered. I knew that was a sign I was no stronger than I had been coming here—rather thin and only with a few noticeable muscles. But I was German. They weren't looking that hard for muscle—they were looking for someone to risk their life so the *Fuhrer* wouldn't have to.

We did this every morning the first day we were here. They insisted we have five minutes each morning to do the 'saluting', or whatever the hell it had been. I was always *unwillig*—reluctant. But I did it anyway. After we went through the drills (which was harder than I ever imagined—up and down the building, carrying guns, up and down, single-file, at attention, *Heil Hitler*, walking around the building, the building again, single-file, up and down, up and down, up and down) we had about ten minutes to eat. I never ate much. The water was nearly literal *schmutzwasser*—wastewater. It tasted like it had come out of a toilet. It was unpleasant trying to swallow it, trying to get it down my dry and closed-up throat. The entire time we weren't drilling—four hours and ten minutes, plus a few extra for the time we got our uniforms on and were allowed to use the toilet (a bucket)—all I thought of was Sharon. *Meine Sharon. Vermisst du so sehr wie ich dich?* I thought every night. *Liebst du mich immer noch, auch durch die Aufgabe, die ich auf meinen Schultern tragen muss?*

When I thought of what could have happened to her and our three children, I couldn't breathe. And I felt weight settle itself in my chest. I remembered the day the German's came—I knew immediately what they were here for. I told them to hide—Sharon was Jewish. What would they do to her if they found her? And then the two officers found me. They took me, no matter if I was "on" their side, fighting for them. The last thing I remember was seeing Tevis's face through one of the windows, where he shouldn't have been. He should have been hiding with his mama. But Tevis was not one to follow much direction. Had they done something to him? *War er lebenig und sicher?* Was he alive and safe?

The weight of my thoughts and worries made a strong ache in my heart. My wanting, dreading heart.

"You," one of the men in the bunks said that night. I could see him on the top of the four-poster. "Are you alone?"

I looked up from writing on a scrap of paper. "*Was?*" I asked. He repeated the question. It was pathetic the second time to my ears.

I thought, and for a second my heartbeat faster as I thought of what I would say. "*Nein. Bin ich nicht.* We're all here, aren't we? Though I had to leave my family behind. I suppose you could say I'm alone."

When we did not speak our *muttersprache*—our mother tongue—we had thick accents. I had always preferred English to German anyway. Not that I could speak it without being looked down on—after all, it was 1939 in Nazi Germany, what would you expect if you began to speak *Englisch?* Since me and Sharon had not taken as kindly to the German language as we did the English one, I had spoken a lot of it in the last ten years. I had always wondered at first why she would have married me, being a German, and forbidding my own mother tongue, but when I said so—once, and once only—she said it was because I was different from the rest, and I was different towards her. I was. I hadn't detested her when I met her, and I had never detested her or thought I hated her the entire time I've known her. My parents had taught me to hate Jews, but I ignored it now. The man who made our children's shoes was Jewish, and he was a sweetheart-like man. So, I felt anxious about having to go and kill Jews. I would rather die myself than do it—*heiling Hitler* position or no.

The man looked at me with a strange look. I thought he could see right through me. Then I started to waver under his gaze, and he gave me a less-intense look. "You are too skinny still," he said.

You should talk, I thought. But I half-shrugged and turned my back to him, lying down on the hard bunk. After a few months these metal beds were one of my only refuges—besides the dreams. I had a different dream out of about five every night—they all involved men wearing uniforms. I still have them. I understand what they mean now.

I was thirty years old at the time. I had been young in *Erster Weltkreig*—World War I—and I only remembered the bombings Vater leaving to fight... and never returning.

Now, being in a place he had once been in (though probably not the exact one, but close enough), I felt helpless, clueless. I didn't know what I wanted, I just felt... wanting. Something, someone, anything—I wanted it. I knew soldiers had to be *stark*—strong. I sure as *verdammt* did not feel strong. I felt weak, and feeling weak was not something that a German should feel.

NEUGIER!" Lieutenant Raus shouted at us all. "Halt die Klappe und seid aufmerksam, ihr idioten!"

A direct translation of what Raus said— *"Shut up and at attention, you idiots!"*

We all shut up and stood straight as boards. I felt so short against these beasts of men around me. I was short in general. Here I felt like an ant... helpless and liable to get *zerquetscht*.

Squashed.

Right under the boots of Commander Tod. *'Tod'*, as horrible as it sounds, means 'death'. I was as aware of the name as I was the rifle slung over his broad shoulder. And I swallowed down my fear as he looked at me, with a bit of a curt nod.

"Schneider," he said, continuing down the lines of soldiers. I had no time to think of an answer but was sure I shouldn't. How idiotic of me. Until a few seconds went by, and he looked over his shoulder, cleared his throat and walked back toward me. Stopped right there.

Sweat rolled down my back.

"*Schneider,*" he said, with emphasis and force in my name.

I croaked, "Kommandant."

He looked at me down his nose and narrowed his eyes, then continued down the line. A few of the soldiers choked on a laugh until Commander Tod said, voice sharp and loud, "*Halt die Klappe!*"

A direct translation of what Commander Tod said— *"Shut your trap!"*

They shut their traps right away.

I stared right ahead like everyone else. My legs were stiff and sore. As were my arms. One of the men in the bunks kept moaning about his arms and his shoulders and his hands and fingers—he had seriously fallen and landed right on his shoulder. And had tried to catch himself on his hands—he had cut them up and given himself sores because of it. He could hardly drill with his hands all *durcheinander gebracht.* Messed up.

We had been doing our usual marching around the building. I hated this most. It was right next to a ravine, which was full of rocks, all the way up and down. It was muddy and slippery here. I had never been fond of narrow, steep spaces right next to a cliff. Not that I had ever *been* next to one... *bis jetzt.* Until now. But what happened next, I won't EVER forget.

I tripped over a rock, and I slid; I was practically sliding down the side of the cliff. I scrambled, trying to prevent myself from falling in there. Then I did what I probably shouldn't have done. I took my rifle, and I jammed it right into the dirt and rocks in my panic. I was holding onto it right over the ledge that led straight down to several ledges and then into a dark hole inside the ravine. I was trying to keep breathing and pushing myself forward at the same time. I felt chunks of rock digging into my hip from leaning onto the cliffside. Then someone looked over the side and tried putting their hand out to me, but then he and his hand was jerked back. I looked up and saw Commander Tod standing there. He had a sharp look on his face.

"Klettern Sie wieder nach ben," he said, and he disappeared over the lip. I heard him say to the others, *"Marschiere weiter!"* They began walking once more, away from the spot I was dangling.

Oh, God.

My head felt empty as I tried hauling myself up. I could not. I felt some of the rock under my foot crash out from under me, and I slipped down farther. My mind was racing and going numb altogether. My breathing was getting scarce. I stayed there on the side of the cliff, until the sound of the other soldiers died away. I couldn't get back up. Minutes went by, maybe an hour. I was holding onto a large rock and my rifle, still stuck in between rocks and in the ground. I do not know how long I waited for my breath to come back to me. I had to try to get my mind from leaving me completely. I may have been a soldier, but I was not one on the inside. Inside I was panic, and nothing else. *Panik.* One of the few things I knew at that camp.

I finally was able to use my hand holding onto the rock to pull me up some. I felt my heart racing. I slowly—very, very slowly—let go of my rifle. I reached up to grab another piece of rock. I started to pull myself up. I wedged my foot in between two rocks for a toehold, and I clambered onto a bit of a ledge. My heart pounded. Would I make it?

I had just gotten my foot from the toehold when one of the rocks I was reaching up to grab broke and disappeared somewhere in the ravine below me. I tumbled farther than I had before down the cliff—at least ten feet more. I didn't yell or make any noise. All the panic rushed back into me, making me feel sick. And the only thing I could do was pray I made it out.

Bitte, Gott, I thought, my heart feeling about to stop at any second. *Hilf mir. Hilf mir. Bitte. Ich brauche deine Hilfe. Bitte. Hilf mir.* I just wanted out of there alive. I wanted more than anything to get the strength back in my hand from it going numb clenching the rock. I wanted more than anything right now not to be here.

Want. That was all my heart was filled with other than fear. *Want.*

I tried moving my left leg to see if I could get a better toehold, but every time I moved, I was practically exposed to nothing, making it seem like I could fall any second. I just gripped the rock. I did not know how I could move without slipping and sliding down the rocks more. More minutes went by

Then I felt something heavy sitting on my foot—heavy, and un-balanced, like it was strewn all over the place. I looked down at my foot and I opened my mouth, but I could not get any sound to escape me. What I saw was a *schlangen*—snake—coiled up, right on top of my boot.

I could not—would not—move. Especially now with a snake sitting right on top of my foot! *There was no way out of here. Auf keinen Fall.*

I felt so helpless, panicked, horrified and trapped over here that I thought of just letting go, and seeing what happened. But I probably couldn't even fall correctly. And I did not know where everyone else was. They knew I was here.

Practically dangling off the side of a cliff with a snake coiled up on top of my boot.

My breathing came heavy yet shallow—breathing hard and getting hardly any air. My hands shook from fear and trying to hold on to the rock. If I moved my other hand..., would I still be *sicher?*

I moved my hand slowly from my side, and reached it up towards another rock, not quite paying attention to what rock it was, as most of my weight was being supported by a poky branch digging into my side, and the small rock below my foot... the one that the snake had decided to take refuge on. When I shifted the slightest bit, the rock beneath my foot slowly, very, very slowly, started to move. I had my hand all the way up in front of me, and I grabbed the rock right before my toehold decided to crumble. The rock I grabbed was not enough to support my weight, and I fell, about twenty feet lower, onto a large and flat rock (the snake no longer was my problem since it fell way down in the ravine, into that dark and narrow hole).

I landed on my back. I felt something in it crunch.

I let out a yell, and I tried to move. Then I realized with my heart pulsing faster in anger (and much cursing) that my foot had gotten wedged right in between two rocks. I tried moving it, trying to get it out. It wouldn't move.

My next yell involved a scream of *"Ich hasse das!"* and I rolled over onto my stomach, pain shooting right up my back. I said, after spitting out dirt, *"Schieße! Ich habe um Hilfe gebeten das passiert!"*

A direct translation of what I said— "Shit! I ask for help, and this happens!"

Then I heard what I did not think I would. Was that the sound of footsteps? ... and getting closer?

I felt my heart starting to pump faster. It felt like it was in my throat. Then I looked up and saw a long line of soldiers in gray-green uniforms, with the Swastika on the arm. And one beast of a man in front. Commander Tod. I saw them stop after a bark of "*Hut! Aufgepasst!*", and then three people looked over the edge of the cliff.

"You down there!" Lieutenant Raus shouted. "What are you doing? You should have gotten back up nearly an hour ago!"

I called back up, "I slipped. About four times, Lieutenant." How embarrassing.

He frowned and leaned closer to the edge. "*What?*"

"I said—" I cleared my throat and tried using my spit to wet it. (Hard to do when you've got no spit.) "—I SAID I SLIPPED ABOUT FOUR TIMES AND ENDED UP DOWN HERE."

He ducked back away from the edge, and I waited a few seconds, trying to stand. The voices I heard sounded like whispers. My back felt oddly stiff and loose and pained at the same time. I managed to stagger to my feet, then leaned onto the rocks. It was hard to do with my foot twisted and in between some stones. The circulation was being cut off and I could hardly feel my foot. Then I saw Commander Tod, Lieutenant Raus and the SS officer Heusen peering over the edge of the cliff once more.

"Hey, Schneider," Heusen called down, "Kannst du umziehen?"

"I can stand," I shouted back. "It's hard though. *Mein Bein steckt fest.*"

He and the others exchanged looks. Then Heusen called back down, "*Nun, wie im Namen Gottes hast du es geschafft, dass du tun?*"

A direct translation of what Heusen said— "Now how in the name of God did you manage to do that?"

My throat was so tight and dry I could hardly answer. I just skipped over that and said, my voice flat, "*Helfen Sie mir?*"

They exchanged more looks, than they disappeared back over the cliff, and I heard Commander Tod bark at his men, "*Geh weiter!*" I saw them continue to walk, and my heart sank. My mouth went dryer than it was already, and I tried to see if the three who had looked over the cliff were walking with them. I scrambled the best I could with my leg stuck. "*Wohin gehst du?*" I shouted up in panic. "*WOHIN GEHST DU? Ich brauche dich! Hey! Wirst du mich verlassen? Mein Bein steckt fest! Ich kann mich nicht bewagen!*" My words rose to a scream, but no one was there. Only a few soldiers were now visible, and they were disappearing around the corner of the path. I could see my rifle pathetically stuck in the ground nearly forty feet above me, the leather strap dangling. And before I could stop myself, I cursed at the top of my voice, the words ringing out in the ravine. *Ich HASSTE das!*

A direct translation of that means— "*I HATED this!*" And I really did.

CHAPTER THREE

A DIRECT TRANSLATION of what I had shouted up at the commander, lieutenant and the SS— "Where are you going? I need you! Hey! Are you going to leave me? My leg is stuck! I can't move!"

I was left out there even after the sky was dark. I could no longer feel my leg. Not just my foot, but my leg. I couldn't break it free of the rocks—I couldn't move more than about twelve inches all ways to grab anything. Not that there was something I could use down here anyway. I had my pistol but that probably wouldn't do something. And I wasn't a very good shot either—I'd probably miss and get my foot instead. Or the bullet would rebound and hit me somewhere else. That and my rifle was about thirty feet above me.

But of course, that was just my *zufall*—my luck. I was starting to feel like I would be trapped down here for the next week if they didn't come back. My foot would probably have so much circulation cut off it fell away. I tried not to think of what might happen then. I wondered what time it was. I had a watch, but it was so dark out here that I couldn't see it anyway.

But there was something about this ravine and being stuck down here in the dark with a very slight wind and the moon faint up there in the black sky, that made me feel slightly less alone. Then I whispered the words, my voice dry and raspy, *"Stille Nacht... h-heilige Nacht... alles ist ruhig—alles ist hell..."*

It was that Christmas song. *Stille Nacht.* Though I supposed the Americans and everyone who didn't speak German just said Silent Night in a normal American accent.

If someone else were to speak English I would probably say, "Ugh, *dummes Englisch,*" but I couldn't. It didn't matter if it was stupid or not. That was what Sharon wanted to speak...

More of an ache than what could ever go through my back went right through my heart. *Sharon... meinem Leibe. Ich vermisse dich bis ans Ende der Welt.*

I couldn't think of if they were *sicher*—safe—or not.

That was when something—or perhaps someone—whistled, and then something long and thin flopped down the side of the cliff, hitting me at first so that I started. Then I heard someone say, there voice hushed but loud in the quiet night,

"Schneider? Schneider, bist du da? Lebst du noch?" A direct translation of what Heusen said— "Schneider? Schneider, are you there? Are you still alive?"

CHAPTER FOUR

MY HEART LEAPT INTO my throat.

"*Ja!*" I called back up. "Yes, I'm still here!" I couldn't believe it! What the heck was he doing here? And after he hadn't done anything earlier? Then something bright and nearly blinding after being in the dark poured over the lip of the cliff. It was a flashlight. The white light got me full in the face, and I squinted, though I could see Heusen's muscly but short frame behind the light. He looked over the edge and his face split into a relieved smile.

"Oh, my God, you're alive!" he said, sounding like he had doubted it earlier. "You're still alive! Are you stuck?"

I looked at him, though I had to strain my neck and lean more to the left to see him. "Yes, I'm stuck. Also... what are you doing here?"

Heusen looked left and right, as if making sure no one was there. "After they vouldn't get you out I decided to come at night to get you. See the rope? Grab it. Let's see if we can get your foot unstuck by pulling you."

I felt my face fall, but I did as he said. I knew there was no way pulling me using a rope would get my foot unwedged from two rocks. But I was grateful he had come when no one else would.

Heusen tugged on the rope. He fiddled with the flashlight, then put the handle end into his mouth, keeping it secure between his teeth and shining it down on what he was doing. "How'd you fall?" he said (I think that's what he said, I could hardly make it out for the flashlight between his teeth) as he pulled more on the rope. I was moved some, but my foot was still wedged between rocks. I didn't feel anything—there was just no circulation left in my leg.

"Tripped," I said, "and then fell. Right off the side of the cliff... I couldn't get back up. I kept slipping farther down..." A piece of rock jabbed me right in the knee. I winced. The rope was still tugging. My foot was still stuck.

"Heusen, it's not working," I said. "I don't think you're going to get my foot out this way."

"How much can you move?" Heusen said, finally taking the flashlight out of his mouth. I could see some spit had dripped out onto it.

"Not much. Maybe a foot left-and-right." Then I thought. "A foot, left and right..." I don't know why I thought it was funny. Without thinking I started laughing. After a few seconds I choked it down. "Sorry."

"Hm." Heusen was thinking. "You got anything down there that'll help get your foot unstuck?" At this I became serious again.

"Nein," I said. "Nichts. Nichts, was ich gebrauchen kann."

"Is that your rifle I see?" Heusen asked, shining his light on the odd shape sticking out of the ground. The way he said it sounded clear, then it faded. Then he yelled and pulled his pistol out of his belt, and as he did so the rope slipped out of his hand. I heard the sharp crack of his gun, but when the rope was released from his hand I fell. But this time—

—my foot came free.

Leider. Unfortunately.

There was a loud *crack,* and pain shot right up my foot. The numb feeling went away, and it was replaced with searing pain. I stumbled back from the shock and then tried to grab something—anything at all—to keep me from going right over the edge. I was unsuccessful and then landed on another platform-like bit of rock a good seven, eight feet below. It was pitch dark down here, and I was cursing from the pain in my foot and that I was now a good eight or so feet from freedom again. I began to stand when I heard a hiss. Then another. They were snarling hisses. I froze. Then I realized, from the faint light the moon gave, that the ground seemed to be moving. Another hiss came and I called out.

Schlangen. Snakes.

CHAPTER FIVE

HEUSEN! HEUSEN, ARE you okay? What happened?"

My voice shook. Shook like my hands. And my leg. The way the ground seemed to quiver beneath me... the snakes *gezittert*. Quivered. And I could feel them slowly slithering around me, at my feet. It must have been around fifty *schlangen*. Then I heard Heusen's call from way above me:

"Schneider? Oh, damn—Schneider! where are you?" His voice was a shout.

"I'm down here!" I said, my voice louder. I heard the snakes hissing at my feet. Heusen must have heard them too because I could tell he froze.

"What was that?" he said. I saw the beam of his flashlight hit the spot where I had been. Then his voice grew panicked. "Where are you?"

"Down here... my leg came loose—I fell again." I was hit with some of the beam from his light, but I could tell he couldn't see the snakes—the ledge wouldn't allow it. Then I felt something begin to wrap around my ankle, the one that wasn't hurt. I caught my breath. I called up, my voice panicked, *"Hier unten gibt es Schlangen! Schnell! Sie bewegen sich—sie versuchen, auf mich zu kommen!"*

A direct translation of what I said— "There's snakes down here! Quickly! They're starting to climb up my leg."

Heusen must have had more rope on his end; he lowered it more, and I could see it start to slither like one of these snakes down off the rocky surface, over the ledge, and finally about a foot above the ground. I reached my hand out and grabbed it. I felt another snake start to make its way over my boot and begin to wrap itself around my ankle. My leg with the hurt foot (which I'm sure was broken at the time) was just hovering above the ground. I shook my other leg and with much hissing the two snakes fell away. I could hear the others' rustling as they moved. It made my stomach twist itself into a knot, and against my better judgment, tears of aggravation and panic were starting to flood my eyes, thinking about if I never got out of here. *Verdammt, verdammt, verdammt!*

Heusen said, "Ready? Try using your leg to find a toehold!"

I felt around until I found rock. Solid rock! I put my foot on it, praying it wasn't a hole that snakes were residing in. When nothing came out and grabbed or sank its fangs into my foot, I called back up, "Ready."

He tugged on the rope for a second, then began pulling with all his strength. I pushed off with my good foot, and he kept pulling. I found another place to put my foot and pushed up from there. He pulled and I found small toeholds, pushing off from them, until I got to where I had been before. I rested my feet on the slab of rock and said, "Take a break."

I let go of the rope and grabbed onto a large piece of rock I had not been able to reach earlier. It kept me from falling. Moving hurt, and my back was still sore. I hoped I had not done something that bad to it. It had cracked when I fell, and I had been in pain because of it nearly the rest of the time I was down there.

After a minute or two of resting Heusen tugged on the rope and I grabbed on, and we repeated what we did before—he pulled, I found toeholds and pushed off from them with my good foot. Several minutes—it took a long time to do this—I was at the spot where I had stuck my rifle into the ground. Heusen shone his flashlight on it (it was in his mouth again, the dope!) and I found a bit of rock to stand on. That small branch of that tree growing up through the rocks was also keeping me from falling backwards. I grabbed the rifle and pulled. After a few more tries it came right out of the ground. I don't know how I got it to stick right in there so well—it was probably the only thing that had kept me falling right down the cliff and into the ravine and dying straight away. (Sometimes when people are desperate, they're capable of doing things they couldn't do any other time.) Once more Heusen pulled on the rope and I walked with my good foot, the rifle over my shoulder.

When I got back up, I stumbled out onto the muddy path, and Heusen leaned back onto the ground. I did the same. My head felt like it was smashed in two and light at the same time. My leg was painfully numb, and my back was aching from being in such an awkward position and landing flat on it on solid rock. My mouth was so dry I could hardly open it to say anything. Then I saw a few bullet cartridges lying around and what appeared to be a long, thin black rope. A snake. That was what Heusen had been shooting at. It was dead.

Suddenly Heusen said, sitting back up, "Your leg okay?"

I shook my head. I knew he couldn't see it. "*Nein. Et ist nicht.*" My voice came out dry, raspy, choked and higher than it should have been. Except for the last couple of minutes, I hadn't realized exactly how thirsty I was. Even that water that tasted like it had come out of a dirty toilet bowl sounded nice to me. I could hardly move. I had been standing with my leg twisted and stuck, and a bunch of rock digging into me, and hardly able to do anything but half-stand, half-sit.

Me and Heusen looked at each other. I could see his face from the moon and his flashlight. He had a small beard, and hair that was as short as mine now. We all had had our hair nearly shaved away. His was dark brown and beginning to turn gray in places. The corners of his mouth just barely lifted. I hoped mine did too. But I could feel my head spinning, and my eyes felt like they were far back in my skull—they felt crowded. My leg was aching, was it broken? Was it just my ankle? I didn't know. Everything was hot out here. My mouth was dry, unbearably dry, and my throat was still tight. My heart was beating faster than it ever had. It didn't seem to want to stop soon. But it must have stopped at some time.

Because I passed out.

I passed out smiling deliriously, so he told me, and mid-laugh.

Right next to Heusen.

CHAPTER SIX

THE NEXT DAY, MY HEAD was still spinning.

My leg hurt so bad I could hardly walk. I don't know how many times Commander Tod came to me and gave me what I suppose he thought was a stern look. I smirked.

He was just glad one of his men weren't dead.

After a long day (too long, it seemed) we were finally in the bunks. I couldn't get that numb feeling inside me to go away. I just kept thinking of how I had been out there, with no one. How I was left out there. And the snakes trying to get up my leg. That was one of the things that made me shudder when I thought of it.

"You could be shocked," Heusen whispered. His voice was concerned sounding to me.

"I suppose. I wish I knew how long I was out there... on the cliff."

This made me start to calculate the hours. We had started walking at five-thirty... and I didn't know what time it had been when Heusen came to get me. I asked him.

"Maybe midnight," he said. "Maybe later. People were already getting into the bunks. Midnight." I had been out there for nearly eight hours.

Heusen said, "I thought you were dead when you fainted."

"Oh," I said, and then grinned. "Of course, I wasn't dead. Were you scared?" I started laughing. Heusen rolled his eyes.

"No," he said, snorting. But he started laughing too until an angry hiss came from somewhere in the depths of the bunks.

"Shut up over there, I'm trying to sleep!"

Me and Heusen grinned at each other and fell asleep shortly after.

I had this thing where I thought if I could write a letter, and send it to Sharon, the words I would say would be, "Do you miss me? Are you alright, are you safe?"

I imagined she was safe. It helped me, thinking. I knew she could be at a death camp right now. That thought always trailed behind my first one, bringing the hard blow of reality to me. And it hurt. The hurt was more than I can ever say.

More and more months went by. We fought. We fought hard, and so many Brits' and Americans' blood was on my hands. I was more exhausted and aching in those months, years, more than I thought I ever would. I had not found Sharon, or our children, and I feared that meant the worst. Sometimes I couldn't control my worries, and they got so intense that I wasn't sleeping or eating or hardly anything at all. You weren't supposed to marry Jews, but I wasn't a regular German of 1940, and since I had married a Jew, I intended to worry about her. Heusen was still alive. I was still alive. Thousands, millions of Jews, and maybe my family, were dead. Hitler was still alive. I wondered what would happen if I put a bullet or two in his head. It didn't matter I was *technically* in his own army—I still hated him. I wanted to kill him. Many wanted him dead and would be brimming with glee to kill him themselves.

Over the last five years my thoughts had turned vicious. Everything, and everyone, seemed in my way. All but Heusen. I was a strong and worrying mess. I had survived the first five years of the war, the *Krieg,* but there could be years ahead. I had been on the submarine U-14, the one that sunk *The Royal Oak* cargo. Me and the others watched it sink, watched men and boys jump out into the water while black smoke poured from the ship. Two torpedoes did it. I had never seen a boat sink from being torpedoed.

I saw so many drown.

There was one refuge, my one redeeming moment, when I could look out and see the mountains and fields and oceans and sky and know that they would always be the same. That those things didn't care about what lived and died. That they didn't have feelings to mourn over losses. And that God was up in that sky... maybe Sharon was up there.

We were in a ditch. It was a muddy, sloppy one. The French had another ditch to themselves. Guns were poking over the ledges of the ditches. My heart thudded somewhere in my throat. Heusen was next to me, lying flat with his rifle just over the top of the edge. We looked at each other. it was the look we exchanged before the shooting. The fighting. The killing. It said that we wouldn't forget each other if the other one died. I nodded. Heusen gave me the slightest smile in return. Then we looked back at our rifles. Waiting for someone to take the first shot. I could hear men breathing next to me. I felt my own breathing—shallow and rancidly choppy. Then an earsplitting crack came from just beside me.

Heusen had just fired.

Germany had just started the gunfight.

  NAOMI LEE REID

It was going to be a bloodbath.

Everyone began firing, the sounds echoing in my ears even through the helmet. I pulled back the trigger to my own rifle and saw one of the several in the opposite ditch fall back with blood flowing from their heads or chests. My heart pounded sickeningly as it always did. Gunfire was the only sound for hours. My ears rang. Tons of our dead men were sprawled on the ground. Soldiers kept firing. Fighter airplanes screamed overhead, shooting at anyone and anything they could find. Until one bullet went right next to me.

Everything seemed to get slower. Time seemed to be slowing down. I saw that bullet shoot past and hit Heusen in the chest. I felt a yell build up inside me and escape as he fell to the ground, lifeless. All I could do was stare at his body.

"*HEUSEN!*" I screamed, but no one heard it. The gunfire was too loud, and I stared at his body, unable to comprehend that he was dead.

I shouldn't have been looking down.

Sudden white-hot pain got me in the shoulder. It hurt for a second, then disappeared. I staggered back from the force, and when I hit the ground so much pain went through my left side—all up my arm, my fingers, my shoulder—that I stared up at the gray sky, unable to move. I shook. Blood was beginning to seep through the green gray of my uniform. My breathing was heavy and hollow. I moved my head the slightest bit to the right and saw Heusen's body lying there. His eyes were lifeless and glassy, staring in my direction. The gunfire seemed to fade from my mind, and everything went quiet. Until I felt someone tugging on me. "Schneider. Schneider. It's over. It's over."

I looked up and saw Raus standing over me. His face swam blurrily in my eyes, which watered from the pain and the weight, the crushed feeling, of losing my friend. My breath came out in gasps. *Heusen's dead. Your friend's dead.* I hadn't ever thought of Heusen as much of a friend before. More of an acquaintance... but he had been a friend.

I couldn't move. My eyes were watering so violently that I could hardly make out the blurred figures standing over me. I felt hands lifting me up, getting me off the ground. The pain made me close my eyes, shutting them tight. When I opened them, I was in the back of a truck. The truck was moving. And I was alone... Alone again.

My eyes watered up once more when I remembered that Heusen was dead. This time, being alone, I let them build up until they ran beyond my control.

Maybe hours passed by. I fell asleep, the pain too much to bear. When we got back to base, they cleaned the place I'd been shot. It hurt so horribly I remember passing out screaming at the top of my voice. It was a mess. I remember blood still seeping through even after they'd put pressure on it, hoping that less blood would flow. It didn't exactly work. Bled for twenty-four hours, I did. until I suppose my shoulder didn't have any more blood left to bleed.

The ache in my shoulder was so bad I could hardly move without pins and needles going right through me. I had to stay in the tent Muller —who oversaw all things medical—was in. Thirty others were here. They were in the same state as I was, though I was sure the biggest one was going to die. I'd seen plenty of the symptoms to know when someone was going to kick the bucket.

About halfway through the night, I jerked awake. Someone was touching me with rather poky fingers. I saw it was Müller. He said, putting a tin cup on the table, "Should've given you this earlier. Drink it."

"What is it?" I said, taking it, feeling dizzy and sick.

"Whisky."

I took it down in one shot. That helps when you're trying to get it down a tight throat... just tip it back. Straight back.

He looked at it approvingly and went back to the beefy man in the corner. At some time, I fell asleep again, but I awoke to the sound of rustling inside the tent. My eyes opened to slits and I saw Commander Tod, Lieutenant Raus and Müller at his cot. Then I saw them put the sheet over his head... and I knew that that soldier was gone.

A stab of grief hit me hard in the chest. I swallowed. *Das ist es Krieg.* That is war. People die and people live, and some go missing and never return.

When I was able to move, and my shoulder had stopped bleeding, I went out of the tent, though Müller wasn't that happy about it (he thought everyone needed a solid week before leaving the tent and clucked and fussed like a mother hen about it). The base was as it was the last time I saw it—though the last time I was a bleeding mass of grief and hardly able to see it through watery eyes caused by the aching sting in my shoulder and the one I felt in my heart.

I would know when someone would be informed that their kids or their spouse was in a death camp, because they would usually walk around with hallow, empty eyes. The Allies were bombing camps and imprisoning other Germans. If the families of Germans weren't in British work camps, they were dead from bombings by the Allies.

Where me and Sharon lived it wasn't uncommon you would walk by a Jewish-owned building with its door nailed shut, and it would have JUDEN painted over the windows and the sides of the building, and then it would sometimes have a swastika on the door, showing that it was no longer a Jewish-owned building, but it was now a German one.

I hoped that Sharon, Nikita, Tevis and Heinrich were safe... I would be destroyed if they weren't. If they were not—I couldn't think about it.

My shoulder was still sore, and I couldn't move my arm as well as I would have wanted; when I did my shoulder started aching. But when you were a soldier, you had about a day to recover.

There was noise coming from one of the tents, and I ducked inside. The smell of cigarette smoke, sweat, stale blood, and pure German males wafted into my face, and the scent of what was unmistakably bratwursts. Several of the men were at an old rickety table with a bunch of cards lying around. They looked up when I came in, and they broke out grinning. I didn't know why.

I was surprised to see that Lieutenant Raus was there.

"Thought we nearly lost you," he said. "Would've been a shame."

I said, "Because you would've been one man short?" Lieutenant snorted. I smirked. That was probably why. But what he said clarified I was wrong.

"*No,*" he said. "Hell, you're one of the best... but don't tell Heinrich, he'll beat you to death if you do."

Everyone laughed at that, and so did I, though it was kind of awkward and nervous. Heinrich was about the toughest person I knew. He could probably rip me in half given the chance. But the name Heinrich made me think of my son, and that didn't leave a very good feeling behind.

After a while I got dragged into the card game, a cigarette, which I'd been longing for since I'd been stuck in Müller's tent, and into two schnapps, which beat that toilet water.

A direct note of what Lieutenant Raus said years after this—*"Yeah, it was real toilet water."*

CHAPTER SEVEN

SOMETHING HAPPENED a month later that I'll never forget. And it was something that brought me back to my family.

We were in Germany, as we had been for the last couple of months. Some of us were at base. And then two of the soldiers came in with two people, dragging them by the arms and hair. When I saw them, my world went blank. And it felt like I was falling through the floor.

I couldn't move.

"We found these two outside the trucks," one of them said, gripping Nakita harder by her hair. Nakita didn't struggle. But her face was white, and a pale, gray-looking green. Tevis was being held still by the arms and the base of his neck by the other soldiers' hand. The one with the rat face said, nastily, *"Der ist Juden, Kommandent."*

Commander Tod looked at them with his blue eyes. "Hm." He walked closer, inspecting them. "Let go of the girl." Nakita was let go and slid to the floor, paralyzed from fear. She stared up at him through her dark brown eyes, which were leaking tears. Commander Tod said, voice cold and soft, "Stand up."

Nakita didn't. My heart seemed about to stop. I couldn't breathe. I couldn't move. I was frozen and couldn't do anything.

Commander Tod's face went hard. "Get up!" he barked, and when Nakita didn't, he pulled his pistol out of his belt, and was aiming right for her, about to pull the trigger—

"NO, WAIT!"

Everyone froze. The word rang around the room. It had been a scream at the top of my lungs. Commander Tod looked around. His gun was still pointing in Nakita's direction. His eyes fell on me. "Schneider," he said quietly. "Get over here."

I walked, breathing hard. Tevis and Nakita finally saw me, and their mouths flew open, but they didn't say anything.

Commander Tod looked at me when I reached him. "You know them?" he said, his voice still quiet and deadly.

"I—" I swallowed. "They're mine."

The whole room seemed to exchange looks. I looked at Tevis and Nakita. Then I looked back at Commander Tod. I said, my voice ringing out in the room, "They're mine and you can't kill them."

The commander stared at me. "They're yours?" he spat. "They're Jews. You're a traitor for marrying and breeding filth, Schneider." Then he lowered his gun. He said, "Let go of the boy." Tevis was thrown onto the floor, right next to Nakita. I ran to them, we collided, and we fell to the floor. They threw their arms around me, and I held on tight to them. *"Meine Kinder. Warum bist du hier? Wo sind deine Mutter und Heinrich?"* I whispered to them, and Tevis whispered back, *"Wir Wissen es nicht.* We don't know." I could hear him crying, and his sister. "We haven't seen them since the day they were taken. The same day as you."

"Vater... wir haben dich vermisst," Nakita said, her voice carrying out on sobs, and I held onto them tighter. I would never let go of them. "We missed you. We needed you."

"I've needed you this whole time," I said, feeling tears running down my face as we sat there, holding onto each other. The rest of the people around me didn't matter. They were erased from my sight. All I could see was my two children, feeling happier than I had in the last four and a half years, and worried that they didn't know where their mother or youngest brother was. And terrified of what might happen now. After a minute I wiped my eyes, I stood up, Tevis and Nakita clutching my hands. I looked at Commander Tod.

"*Lass mich sie nehmen,*" I said. "Let me take them."

Commander Tod's mouth opened. "You can't just—you—" he began, his tone angry.

I said, my voice rising, "They're mine and you'll let me take them."

I had never felt so angry and scared in my life. He couldn't tell me I couldn't take my own *kinder,* my own kids. And I was going to, even if he said I couldn't. Because I could; I was going to get them and myself out of here. Even if we had to run and hide.

Commander Tod looked at me with his cold eyes. Everyone in the room was watching him, their leader. And the movement he made was quick—he pulled out and pointed his pistol at me, but I was quicker and shot him right through the head. He dropped to the ground, dead, blood pouring, and before anyone could think to do anything but fumble for their guns, Tevis and Nakita and I were running.

Oh, hell, yes. We were running.

CHAPTER EIGHT

WE RAN AND RAN, HEARING people behind us firing their guns, the bullets missing us. When another blast would sound Nakita screamed, and Tevis would yell at the top of his voice. We kept running, until we got to the place where I had been trapped nearly five years ago. We could hear trucks and people shouting out in German.

I looked at Nakita and Tevis. "We're going to hide," I said, and I grabbed them and pulled them closer to the edge. I had been down here once, and I was going down again—I had to hide them. I stepped on a flat piece of rock, and they stepped down too. We stumbled down a good way, until the rocks made us slide; we half-staggered and half-ran, going down until we got to a flat piece of rock. It was the one I had been trapped on for hours, and below it was a hole that led straight down. I looked over the edge and saw that it wasn't that far—and there was water inside. It looked deep enough, if you jumped you might still live. Tevis saw what I was looking at and looked about to scream. I grabbed them both by the shoulders.

"Listen to me," I said, breathing hard like them. "Listen. I don't want you to be killed by them. You must follow me. We're going down there. You need to do what I say. Do you understand?" They nodded their heads fearfully. I jumped down onto the ledge, and they clambered down with me. I told them that when I said to jump, they must jump into the hole, and not make any sound. Just stay still and wait for me.

When I heard the trucks rumble to the top of the cliff, I saw people run to the side, their guns pointed in front of them at us. I said, "*Jump!*" to Tevis and Nakita, and without hesitation they leapt. They fell into the hole, and I heard Nakita's shriek as they were engulfed by the darkness and the loud slosh of water. I looked at the cliffside and saw one of the soldiers pull the trigger to his rifle. The bullet struck the ground only feet from me. I pulled my pistol from my belt again and shot at the three standing there; they yelled and fell to the ground, one of them tumbling down the side of the cliff and rolling until he disappeared. More and more gunshots followed, and the bullets hit the rocks and dirt by me; I shot out at them four times until I jumped, being swallowed by the darkness and the water that lapped and splashed over me.

CHAPTER NINE

WHEN I CAME BACK UP Tevis and Nakita were already out of the water, Tevis's shirt sticking to him and Nakita's dress floating. The water in here made a clinking sort of echo as it went still. The water was cold, but not freezing. The green-gray color of my uniform was nearly the same color as the water, and the material stuck to me. Patterns in the color gold were on the rocky walls. I slowly made my way to Tevis and Nakita. We were all soaked after diving in. We stayed pressed against the rock. I held them back with my arms. It was dark in here, and quiet. I wonder how long the water had been in there. The water gently splashed us, making our clothes wetter.

I could hear their hard breathing. My own breathing was heavy. When we couldn't hear the soldiers anymore, I looked at them. And I wrapped my arms around them, and they did so to me. After a few long minutes that could never make up for nearly five years of being alone and away from them, I let go. I looked at the back of the cave. There was a tunnel, I could see, and it was higher above the ground than this area was. There was some water in it, but not much. It was big enough that we could stand. We swam across the dark water, and I could see an even darker spot beneath us as we got to the middle. A cave underneath this one... I wonder how deep it went.

When we got to the other side we stood up on the barely wet pebbles. We were dripping. Nakita's dark hair was stringy and sticking to her face and neck, and her dress hung soaked and limp at her knees. Tevis's pants and shirt were sticking to his body and his boots squished; his hair was flopped over his face and dripping water. So was mine, making a bit of a sound when the drops hit the rocks, echoing in the cave.

We kept walking. We were all short enough that we didn't have to crouch the slightest when the ceiling got to be low. The bit of water sloshed when we took steps. I think Nakita kept looking for snakes, peering into the dark corners of the tunnel. When the water got to be a little deeper, first by a few inches to a foot and a half, the temperature dropped drastically. It was boiling hot out above the ground, but down here, with the water, it was about thirty degrees cooler.

After a while Tevis said, his voice loud in the silence (except for the water swishing at our feet), "Um... how come you never came home?"

I slowed for a second, but then went my normal pace. I had been dreading this question from the start; from the times I imagined when I was able to return home. I swallowed. "I couldn't," I said at last. "I was trapped."

"How?" Nakita said, bunching her sopping skirt in her hands so it didn't get caught on any rocks. I felt the smallest smile—so small it probably only shone in my eyes, not my face—and took a deep breath.

"It wasn't what you might picture," I said. "It wasn't like they tied me down or anything. Because they didn't. But being there, that was what trapped me; and I didn't know where you were or if you were safe or not, and the things I was forced to do..." I paused, feeling these words swirl inside my head. "I had to kill hundreds of people. I saw so many people die, because of me, and I didn't choose to *kill* them." I thought back to what I had done earlier, shooting Commander Tod through the head. I had done that purposely. I had done that, but I did so we could get out. If I hadn't, we could be dead right now. "... and I need you to know that I wasn't just physically trapped. I was trapped in my head. All I knew there was panic, and fear, and I was constantly worrying about you all." I looked at them both. "It was that way for nearly three years—and I couldn't come back."

Tevis looked at me through his dark eyes. "Did you get used to it?"

I frowned slightly. "Yes, but..."

"But?"

"But I never got used to it."

I knew it didn't make sense, at least not to them. But to me it did. I had always tried to get used to that crawling feeling inside me, the way everything was seeming to crumble around me, and I couldn't escape it... not once. I tried to get used to that feeling. It didn't take in those few years, where my heartbeat so fast I thought it would burst, where I could hardly breathe, that sick, wanting feeling

"You're older now," I said, realizing it was true.

Tevis gave me and grin. "Yep. Almost fourteen."

"And I'll be thirteen," Nakita said proudly.

"And I'll be..." I pretended not to know. Nakita gave me a joking sympathetic look and Tevis said, "You'll be thirty-three."

"Right. I'm that old? I'm ancient compared to you two."

After a while longer the water started to get shallower. It was getting roomier in the tunnel. I hoped that the SS officers and the Nazis didn't know there was a tunnel. But I didn't say so. I didn't want to jinx it; the Nazis were probably counting on my luck anyway. My bad luck.

I don't know how long we continued walking. A long time, until inside the tunnel was getting darker than it had been. Nakita was walking ahead. The water had gotten around our knees, but there was still a lot of room left from the top of it to the ceiling. She was about six feet ahead.

She took a step, and the moment she did I knew something was wrong about it. She fell, and disappeared into the water, into a hole inside the tunnel.

CHAPTER TEN

AND SHE DIDN'T COME back up.

In panic we both scrambled to the side, and we could see the dark hole. Something under the dark water was moving—thrashing and kicking out. Hurriedly me and Tevis reached under, and I could feel her hair, but not her. I knew she should have come back up by now, and I quickly got in, dove under and felt in the nearly black water for Nakita.

Something kicked me, right in the leg. Was it Nakita? Then I grabbed out in the water and touched her arm. I snatched it and tried pulling. She wouldn't move. I could still feel her kicking in the water, and I felt for her, and clutched the material of her skirt. The kicking was getting less intense, but when I pulled again, this time she moved.

We both came up.

Nakita was soaked once more and pale. She was shaking. I helped her climb out of the hole and onto the rocks, the bit of water sloshing some. I planted both my hands on the rocks and hauled myself out, water streaming down me. Nakita was dripping loads. Tevis was holding onto her wrist. I said, "Are you okay?"

She nodded. "Um—"

I looked down at the hole she had fallen into. "We must be more careful. For now, let me walk ahead. Are you sure you're alright? What happened down there?"

"I c-couldn't get out. My leg was stuck for a minute."

I knew how it felt to have your leg stuck and begin to panic. I asked which leg had gotten stuck and checked it to make sure it hadn't gotten cut any. Her leg only had a scrape, but I knew how scared she had been. I told her it was going to be okay, but I couldn't stop my own thoughts from questioning if there would be more of these holes along the way.

We kept walking until it was the day. And we were having to check the ground every couple of minutes to make sure there weren't any more holes and caves to fall in. While we were walking (the water level ankle-deep) the cave seemed to be getting brighter. We were walking quicker. The cave was getting brighter and brighter until we could hear running water. Then we came out and our eyes were stabbed by sunlight, so bright that it was practically blinding. I could hardly see for it; we'd gotten used to the dark and were in that tunnel for about two days.

When our eyes adjusted (it took several minutes) we began to walk again. I wondered how far away we were from the officers and soldiers. Were they going to come after us? After me? I didn't know. They hadn't followed us, I'm sure; we were alone in the tunnel the whole time.

After another couple of hours (I couldn't use my watch because it had gotten wet too many times—it was now useless) and we came to a field, with a barbed wire fence. A part of it was cut away. Something was coming out of the field in clouds. It was gray. "Is that smoke?" Tevis said, shielding his eyes against the sun.

Me and Nakita looked too. "Oh. That is," I said, and we went through the opening in the fence to investigate it. It was about two hundred feet from the fence, Nakita staggering and letting a groan get through her teeth. The closer we got, we could make out things. There was a fire, two tents, and a motorcycle parked just outside one of them. There were people, five of them.

When they saw us, they stopped what they were doing and jumped up. There was an older woman and two men her age, an older teenage girl and two younger boys. We were about thirty feet from where they were. I had Nakita and Tevis behind me. I was clutching their wrists... in case. Just in case.

The older man shouted, "Who are you?"

I ran my tongue over my dry and constantly peeling lips. Shouted back. "Aldous Schneider."

"You German?"

"Yes."

"You a Nazi?"

"I was. Two days ago."

"Those hostages of yours?"

"They're my children."

We were shouting across the distance. It felt glorious.

"What are you here for?" the man shouted.

I thought. "Saw the smoke," I yelled. "Wanted to come see what it's from."

He and the others exchanged looks. The woman had pushed her children in the larger of the two tents. The other man was slowly moving towards the motorcycle. My eyes narrowed. The one who was talking—shouting at us—said, his accent thick, "How do we know we can trust you?"

"Don't know," I shouted back. "Can I trust *you*?"

I could see out of the corner of my eye that Tevis and Nakita thought this a good point, because they looked at each other with a bit of an amused look on their red-cheeked faces. Sweat was dripping down my temple and my back. I'd taken off the jacket and left it underneath a bush over by the fence. Nakita had left her sweater with it. The sleeves of her dress were rolled up, and those of Tevis's shirt. It was scorching out here. I don't know how hot, but it was boiling. I wouldn't have minded being I that cave or the tunnel soaking wet right now—beat cooking in the August sun.

I knew that Nakita might be close to fainting soon. She kept moaning and saying her head hurt and was light at the same time as we walked. She had tripped over nothing several times. Her head sort of lolled instead of looking up straight. She was leaning into me.

I said, to the man, "You got water?"

He seemed to think. I wondered if he muttered something to his wife, or whoever she was, because I saw his lips move and she said something to him. Then he called back, "Your girl doing okay?"

He meant Nakita. "No. Think she might pass out soon." Nakita didn't seem to notice this. Only a minute ago she had been giving Tevis looks, and now she could barely lift her head up to see the man walking towards us. Nakita started to go limp, leaning farther into me. The man was about ten feet from us when she crumpled altogether. I caught her and held her off the ground. Her face was bright red, and she was sweating so much the drips were going down her face, not just staying on her skin.

The two of us—the man and me, as Nakita was officially swooned—had to lift her up and bring her to the spot where the tents were. The woman said, "*Wat is er gebeurd?*" I had no idea what she was saying.

"*Flauwgevallen,*" the man said. I didn't know what he said. She nodded. She turned but caught sight of me and Tevis. Her eyes slid from my arm up to my bicep. "*Waar is je hakenruis? Zei je dat je een nazi bent?*" she said. I stared at her, unable to understand what she had just asked.

The man responded to her, seeing my hesitation, "*Hij spreecht geen Nederlands, Ginevra.*"

The woman sniffed. When she spoke her accent was thick, like she didn't speak English enough to pronounce her words right. "Did you say you were a Nazi?"

Her voice grew a little anxious.

"I left base today," I said, looking at her. I knew she didn't trust me. I couldn't say I trusted her. "They had Nakita and Tevis, wouldn't let me take them, and we ran."

"So they're after you."

"The commander is dead."

"How did he die?" Her tone was suspicious.

I looked back at Nakita and brushed her sweaty hair out of her face. "Killed him."

She sniffed and disappeared into the larger of the two tents. After a minute the teenage girl stepped out of the tent, and the look on her face went from scared to blank and then to sweet. I felt suspicious about her. I'd watch her.

The woman came back out with water. She said, "*Voor het meisje...*"

I couldn't understand her again—she wasn't speaking German—but I wondered, by the way her hands trembled, if she had done something to the water. Clearly, she wanted me to give it to Nakita. Before I gave it to Nakita, I took some of it myself. Tasted normal. It was cold. It could still have something in it. If they poisoned her...

I awoke Nakita and she stared up at me through her sweaty eyelids. Her lips were parted so I could see the tips of her teeth. Her eyes were half-closed. I said, voice soft and quiet, "Nakita. *Nakita, morgen, Leibling. Wasser.*" She let out a sigh and her eyes opened some more. I showed her the water. "*Nakita. Wasser.* Drink it. There you go." She took it a small bit at a time. Tevis was watching, sitting very close to where I was. The place was very smoky. How could they have a *fire* going in this heat?

Then I knew why. There were bunches of mosquitos flying around, so they were using the smoke to kill them; and they were also cooking. I tried to ignore the empty feeling in the pit of my stomach, and I think Tevis was too. Watching Nakita drink the water made me realize how dry my mouth was. Being surrounded by water in the tunnel had made it feel like we were hydrated enough—being out in the heat made us realize we weren't.

But the man—the one who had been calling to me—gave us a canteen. I looked in it. It was full of water. I handed it to Tevis and he without hesitation drank a good deal of it. Then he gave me a bit of a guilty look and handed it back to me. I drank some of what remained. Handed it back to the man. He pushed it back at me.

I gave the rest to Nakita.

"Is it just you three?" he asked, sitting cross-legged on the ground. I waited a second, giving Nakita more of the water, before responding.

"Yes," I said. "My wife and youngest son... I don't know where they are."

"Since when?"

"Nearly five years."

He looked a little uncomfortable talking to me. He fidgeted a little with the buttons on his shirt. He brushed his hand through his brown hair. "*Ben je Duits?*"

I stared at him. I didn't know what that meant, whatever language that was. He repeated his question. "You're German, right?"

"Yes. You?"

"Dutch."

"I suppose I've invaded your country then."

After a long time, maybe around three hours, Nakita had finally gotten her strength back and could stand and walk. The Dutch insisted we eat, but I didn't touch anything. Tevis had a small bit. Nakita had mainly water and a small bit of bread with ham. I was only thinking of them, not myself, though I was starving and felt like I might die of thirst any second, but I didn't say anything. I hesitantly took about two swallows of water and then put the limit there.

Magnus Raben, as the man introduced himself, was curious about Sharon. I said she was Jewish. He found it odd. I said I didn't salute to the Nazis from choice; I had to do it by force.

"You are an odd German," he said. "Sensible, but odd no less."

Not sure if that was a compliment or an insult—perhaps intended to be both—I just said, "I'm not like them. That's all. And that's the truth."

Later that day, when the sky started to get dark, I said, "We should probably go..."

"What? No! It's late!" The teenager named Kylie jumped up from her perch on the mat set by the fire. I could tell she was beginning to think something of me. She'd been trying to flirt with me, I could tell. I, however, thought it insulting. When she did this I just glared and said nothing. "I could let you sleep on my cot," she said. "I'll just sleep out here."

"*Nee, Kylie,*" Magnus's wife—Ginevra—said, fixing her multiple shawls. Her hair was all piled up on top of her head, with wooden beads rattling every time she shook her head. Her cloth headband held the mass in place. "*Ja slaapt in je eigen bed.*"

"Maar, Mama..."

There was no further argument intended, I knew from the look Ginevra gave her daughter. She was a very stern woman. I wonder if she knew what Kylie was doing.

Trying to get on my good side, were you, Kylie? It wasn't working. I liked her less and less every time she foolishly batted her eyelashes at me.

Most of the people here were dark-haired with olive-complected faces and arms. Probably from being out in this field all summer. Magnus had said that they had been living out here for a few months, and constantly having to leave due to bombings, being followed by Nazis, et cetera. When he said "Nazis" I felt a little uncomfortable, and everyone seemed to inch their way a bit farther from us.

"Well, I won't kill you," I said. "And I won't report you. I left them. It was a prison there... And if they take me again, I'll just have to break out once more."

"You killed the commander?" one of the boys said (they were identical; I couldn't tell them apart) in awe. He said, "Did you kill anyone el—?"

His mama snapped her fingers at the back of his head. He rubbed the spot and stopped talking.

I gave him a look with images of those I'd killed replaying in my mind. "Too many," I said, my voice hollow and dead.

I knew my eyes were glazing over. Everyone saw it and looked away.

The rest of the time I thought of if Sharon was alive and *sicher*, or if she was dead and in a better place. I wanted her to be alive. I *needed* her to be alive.

We ended up staying. Nakita and Tevis had fallen asleep, and I didn't feel up to waking them and making them walk all night. I was too exhausted myself. But I couldn't sleep. I wouldn't. I'd missed enough sleep in the last four, five years of my life that I could shove exhaustion into the corner and stay awake the whole night, not attempting sleep at all. Though I wanted to. *Really wanted to.*

Somewhere around eleven, maybe, or midnight, Magnus came out of the larger tent with two bottles. "Here." He set one on the ground next to my boot. I slowly picked it up, never taking my eyes off him. He rolled his eyes.

"It's whisky, for goodness' sake. You Germans are cautious. Glad I'm not you."

Magnus was just a jerk in general.

I slowly took the bottle and turned it over, then cautiously took the cork out. Magnus looked amused. I shot him a look and drank about half of what was in the bottle in five seconds, letting thirst get the better of me.

Magnus said, "Is it true you German's are good at drinking?"

"I don't know," I said. "Why would you think that? Isn't that like me saying, 'Is it true you Dutch are great at living in windmills?' And I'll let you know for nearly five years the only thing I've drank is literal toilet water. It's rancid. And I've gotten used to it."

"Then I suppose you consider this a gift from the lord above," Magnus said, smirking a bit as he drank.

"Of course not." I looked at the remaining whisky inside the wide bottle in my hands. I swirled it around. "A long time ago, perhaps. But now..."

He shrugged. "It's the war. People always lose faith in the war."

"The *Krieg* has got nothing to do with it," I said, snapping a bit.

"The creek?" Magnus said, confused. "What creek? The one nearly three hours back there?" He pointed left, behind him.

"No... the *Krieg,* the war— '*Krieg*' means war in..." I didn't finish. But I did drink more of the whisky, staring off into the dark field. Magnus fallowed my stare and then said,

"What are you looking at?" His voice grew heavy.

"*Nichts.* That is, nothing."

I wonder how much he believed me about that, but it was true. I was just looking at nothing with my eyes, but in my mind's eye I was seeing only Sharon.

I was awake the whole night.

It was around one in the afternoon when suddenly we could hear the hum of an airplane. But then it got louder and louder. Off in the distance, five of them could be seen, massive gray beasts flying this way. Bombers.

CHAPTER ELEVEN

EVERYONE WHO WAS IN the tent came out.

They looked up at the sky, shielding their eyes against the sun. Then they started shouting for the others to hide. They were trying to take down the tent. It wasn't working and the planes were getting closer. Suddenly I grabbed Kylie by the arms and said, having to yell over the wailing of the closing in planes, "Wait! Stop what you're doing!" They did.

"Those are German planes, they're low, and they won't bomb me," I said, hoping it true enough. "Make it look like I'm arresting you. Try running."

They looked at me as if I had gone crazy, which maybe I had, but it was worth trying. I grasped Kylie's arms and began dragging her the best I could. The airplanes got to be deafening as they screamed overhead. Kylie kicked and she let out a scream, and then her mother started to play along and let out a scream too. She began to start forward, but I pulled out my empty gun and pointed it right at her. She froze, and I kept walking, dragging Kylie by the arms, and Kylie continued to kick and scream and thrash, until the planes had disappeared, and the field was left unscathed by the bombs that didn't fall.

I let go of Kylie. Half-throwing her would be better worded, but I wasn't that rough with her. Though, she had kicked me in places no one wants to be kicked, and this was my getting her back.

The other man, Coal, said, over the receding hum of the airplanes, "What made you think that would work?" As every time I heard him talk, he sounded harassed. He always was. I said, putting my pistol with no ammunition back in my belt, "They wouldn't bomb a Nazi. Those were German bombers. I'm a Nazi. Well, was. They probably wouldn't bomb me anyway unless they knew *who* I was." Thinking I should add this, I said, "And when you talk to me"—everyone's eyes got wider "—sound less infuriated, would you?"

Coal's mouth opened, then closed. Then he said, in a mumble, "Yes."

"Gut."

And that was the end of the conversation.

I didn't think we would stay as long as we did. For nearly two weeks, we stayed, until Magnus said, "You know... ah, do got anywhere to be after this?"

I thought. "No. I don't really know where we're going to go after this; I suppose we're still on the run."

"You could stay," he said.

I felt like he had slapped me. Stay? I thought he wanted us out of here! But it had been fine staying... I trusted them a little bit more. Not all the way, but a bit more. It was better than having to go days without drinking or eating, or walking all day and night with two kids who needed the rest and food more than I did. And not knowing where we were exactly, or if we would turn up in a camp full of Nazis. I didn't miss that. What I did miss was Sharon and Heinrich. And home. Though, I didn't know if home was there anymore. If the Nazis had gotten ahold of Sharon, they probably shut up our house and stole everything inside it. And thinking of that made me feel empty, almost sick from the emptiness.

I saw Nakita and Tevis farther in the field with the two boys and Kylie. I could never remember the boys' names either. They asked if we had code names and I said not really, but hostages got numbers tattooed onto their arms. They were fascinated and said they wanted me to put tattoos on their arms. I said I couldn't put a real one on, but we could find some sort of ink. They found one of their father's ink pens and we used that (with Ginevra's permission).

"When were you born?" I asked the one with slightly shaggier brown hair.

He thought until he answered, "About the same time as him." He pointed to his brother. His brother nodded and grinned.

"Any time specifically?" I asked.

"Don't know. We were born on the same day, me and him."

"Who's older?"

When we got that figured out, this was how we did it—year, month, day, initials. On their forearms, in black ink, were the letters and numbers:

3275MSR

and,

3275MAR

They were constantly going around showing off how they had these numbers on their forearms, and then Kylie said she wanted one, then Tevis. I was hesitant to do it, but the Ravens—that is, the family who we were with—thought it was funny. Once the 'tattoos' were done, they all read like this:

Kylie: 2688KLR

Tevis: 28228TAS

Nakita: 29125NSS

"Give yourself one," Nakita said. "That way we all have one!" The looks on all their faces made me sigh and put the numbers and letters on my forearm. When I was done, 3275MSR—that was how I was telling them apart—looked at it and said, "Nineteen nine, June 5, A.D.S. What does A-D-S stand for?"

"Aldous Dietrich Schneider," Nakita said matter-of-factly, pushing her glasses up her nose. I nodded and put the pen in MSR's hand. He knew it meant to go put it back. We were allowed to have it if we put it back afterwards.

"What does Nakita's stand for?" Kylie asked, scooching closer to me. I scooched farther away and said,

"Nakita Sharon Schneider. And Tevis's stands for Tevis Aldous Schneider."

"Oh, Sharon's a pretty name," Kylie said. "Did you think of it?"

"Yes. She's got my wife's name." I put emphasis on the word *wife* and Kylie immediately looked offended and smug. She stood up after a few minutes and went into the tent.

"She likes you, Mister—I mean, Herr Schneider," MAR said. "It's gross." He pulled a face.

"But you're amazing," MSR said quickly.

"Yeah," his brother said. "*You're* amazing, *she's* gross." They looked at each other and started giggling so violently everyone near them started to laugh as well.

Ginevra came over from the fire where she'd been cooking and said, "Now what's so funny?" She put her hands on her hips. Her many fringed shawls swayed in the hot breeze. I wondered how she could wear so many of them when it was nearly a hundred degrees out here.

"Kylie's sweet on Dad," Tevis said, disgusted. I felt disgusted too, hearing him say it.

"Are any of you encouraging her?" Ginevra had a stern look on her face. It wasn't she was concerned about Kylie liking me in general, it was just that I was German. Her eyes slid over to me. I shook my head.

"No," I said, "and I *have* a wife. Kylie understands." *I think.* That part I didn't add. But I knew from Ginevra's pursed lips and glance behind her shoulder at the tent meant that she would be talking to Kylie.

The Rabens had something where they told a story every Saturday evening. Everyone sat around eating while Coal talked about being in the woods and getting so lost, he said he could've been upside-down, and he wouldn't know. When he was finished, there was a small silence where the only thing you could hear was people chewing on the chunks of beef and potato in the soup. Then Magnus frowned and said, not looking at me, "So, Schneider... you got a story?"

I was quiet. I stared into the bright orange flame of the fire and said, "I suppose." I shrugged. *Sweet lord, I'm dying for a cigarette.* "I don't know if I should tell it."

"Go ahead," Coal said. He looked at me through his dark brown eyes. I swallowed and took a deep breath.

"I was at the military camp. Back at that place it was a prison, prison in that building and in your mind. I couldn't escape it. We were taken there, drafted without a choice, and taken. The training was hard. They push you there and they push you to the point where you can hardly catch your breath.

"I wasn't that good of a soldier. The stress was enough that I could hardly move. Everything I did hurt, and all I could think of were Sharon, Nakita and Tevis, and Heinrich. Only them. And it was starting to make me go mad, all that thinking and worrying and hoping... and the wanting.

"Once we were doing the thing we did every day—drill. It was unbearable drilling. Up and down the building, out in the heat or the rain. It had rained recently, and the ground was all rocky and wet and muddy. We were right on the side of a cliff—we did this every day over there, on that path, nearly four hundred men taking it in parts, twice around the path. It took nearly three hours to get all the way around. There was this huge ravine, full of rocks and holes, and it was steep.

"I tripped over some rocks that were in the path, and I slipped, and ended up hanging right over the side of the cliff. I couldn't get back up, and I kept sliding until I stuck the end of my rifle down in the rocks and the dirt. That kept me from falling completely. Someone tried helping me get back up, but Commander Tod told them to leave me. Everyone kept walking, and I was left there; I kept sliding because of the unstable rocks and mud and loose dirt, and I went down farther, about ten feet.

"I could hardly get a toehold down there. My rifle was stuck above me, and I couldn't grab it, because it was too far, and the only thing keeping me from sliding down the whole cliff completely was this old dead tree—it was more of a twig than a tree, and it could've snapped in half, but it didn't. I was panicking so much I couldn't breathe. The others were gone, and I was alone, just hanging there."

I stopped talking. My throat had gone tight. My heart was beating faster, like it had been in the ravine. Everyone was quiet, no longer eating. Kylie said, voice loud in the silence, "How'd you get out?"

"Heu—" The word was cut off by my throat closing. "A—a friend."

I cleared my throat and went back to eating, and so did everyone else. They could see I couldn't finish. But I said, remembering, "There were hundreds of *schlangen*—snakes down there. A few of them started climbing up my leg."

MSR and MAR swapped amazed looks with each other. I saw them do it when they thought I wasn't looking. It made me smile, but it was wobbly. I was still dying for a cigarette.

The heat of the night was not nearly as wretched as in the day. At least there was a bit of a breeze. Nakita and Tevis slept in the smaller tent. I hardly slept at all, and when I did it was outside. Coal, Magnus, Ginevra, Kylie and the boys slept in the large tent. There was enough room that they could fit most of their cooking things inside with them. I wondered where they had gotten the tent; it could have been from the black market.

People were always buying things on the black market. If it meant they got food in their stomachs and a place to sleep, they would go to just about any level—trading things, selling everything they owned, getting things from the black market. Everyone did it, and everyone wouldn't *not* do it.

I was alone outside. I thought of Heusen and Sharon and Heinrich, and such wanting and hurt stabbed at me that I could feel it. No matter where I was, or who I was with, there was always that painful wanting. And the images of the people I was responsible for killing, they were always there. And Sharon and our son—where were they? Were they alive, and safe? I tried to convince myself they were. But every time I did, my aching, wanting, breaking heart shattered some more.

Soldiers, Nazis—even ones who were on the run—were supposed to be strong, and not let the things that they missed and longed for most get in their way.

But did soldiers ever have any shattered hearts and try to hide them?

Did soldiers cry?

CHAPTER TWELVE

IN THE MORNING THERE was someone walking through the field, making their way towards the tents. They were staggering, stumbling, and looking the way Nakita had before she fainted—head lolling, feet dragging, body looking limp.

It was a very hot day—at least a hundred and ten degrees out. We had been staying inside the tents most the time, it was so hot. But Tevis and Nakita, Kylie and the two boys went out, and then stuck their head inside the larger tent and said, "Someone's coming!"

We all went out and could see the person getting closer. The person had long silvery hair, and was thin, almost unnaturally thin. From this far away we could see it was a woman, though she could have passed for a small teenager, she was so short and thin. It was when we saw her fall right over in the field that we began to walk that way, Coal, Magnus, Ginevra, and me. When we got a foot away from her, I saw the woman had a long and thin nose, nearly see-through eyebrows and a long neck. And long, pale eyelashes.

"Angela?" My voice was nearly a shriek. Was this really my sister? What was she doing here? And alone?

We scrambled to pick her up and carried her back to the tents. It was hard from her being limp, but she was so skinny and small we could get her there without dropping her. When Nakita and Tevis saw her they both said, "Is that Tante Angela?" Their expressions were of pure astonishment.

Magnus said, "You know her?"

"This is my sister," I said, unable to believe it. Ginevra rushed to get some water, and she awoke Angela gently.

Angela's head lolled from side to side and her eyes were hardly opening. But she must have caught glimpse of me, because she said, her voice a croaky moan, "Aldous?"

And her eyes closed again.

It was around night when she finally awoke.

Ginevra came to her with water, which Angela drank slowly, as if worried that if she drank it too fast it may not have quenched her thirst. I sat not very far from her. She turned her head in my direction and choked, water spluttering out of her mouth and coming from her nose. Me and Ginevra jumped up while Angela coughed and spluttered. She choked out, "A-Aldous? What are you doing here?"

"What are *you* doing here, Angela?" I said, sitting down next to her while she used her hand to wipe the water she had spit out off her face; she was still coughing, but at least she could talk. Her breath came out in gasps, but it was probably from choking on the water.

"I—I had to run away from Dresden," she said, her face falling and tears welling up in her eyes. "A-Aldous—it's not like it used to be. It's nearly destroyed. When the Nazis—and the bombers—Aldous... I don't know where the older children are..."

"I have Nakita and Tevis," I said hurriedly, and when Angela saw them, she started sobbing so uncontrollably that I couldn't make out what she said next. Or rather, I could hardly get her to say what she said next.

"A-Aldous," she gasped, a shudder running through her entire body, and her eyes still ran with tears. She was shaking. I could see the fear and grief in her eyes. I was scared for what she might say next.

"Aldous... they took Heinrich. They took him to... to..."

My heart was about to stop. I swallowed the panic and fear rising inside me. Angela gave me such a devastated look I wanted to turn away from it.

"They... they t-took him to the d-death camp. In Dachau."

CHAPTER THIRTEEN

MY WORLD SEEMED TO shatter at those words.

I couldn't breathe. A numb feeling took over me. My heart stopped. I couldn't think, couldn't move. Couldn't say anything. My head was spinning.

Then a horrible feeling came over me—crashing like a bomb. It was like what I had felt when Heusen dropped dead beside me. Only this was worse. I staggered to my feet and stepped away from Angela and the Ravens. Nakita and Tevis sitting frozen. I felt my stomach work into knots, so tight it must have been iron. Outside the glow of the fire, where it was cold from the dropped temperature, I shuddered. When I did, I felt my eyes start to burn. There was no way Heinrich was still alive. If he had been taken there nearly five years ago, and no one heard about him, he was dead.

Tears were starting to prick the corners of my eyes. I clamped my eyes shut, and the moment I did, I wanted nothing more than to go and hurt whoever took him.

Over the next few weeks Angela stayed with us and the Ravens. She said she had been with Sharon but ran for it when the Nazis started watching her and Sharon. When she said this, I just stared at her.

"*Spinnst du?* Why would you leave her?" I shouted. Angela looked taken aback but jumped to her feet, much like how I had stood up. I said, my voice just as loud as it had been before, "Why would you leave if you knew the Nazis were watching you both? Why didn't she come with you?"

Angela threw her hands up and said, "She wouldn't come! That's not my fault! Stop yelling at me and just listen to what I've got to say!"

She didn't raise her voice. Of course. Angela had always been quiet and calm, and barely spoke louder than a mutter. No wonder our parents had played favorites.

I crossed my arms and looked at her harshly. She shrank slightly at the intensity of it but said, "Sharon wouldn't come with me. I asked over and over; I *begged,* Aldous—she wouldn't listen, wouldn't come. I'm sorry—I wanted her to come with me. I felt horrible leaving her behind. I haven't seen her for nearly a year."

This information played inside my head until I found the odd thing about it. My heart beat faster and faster as I thought about it...

"Nearly a year?" I said, my voice quick and higher than it should be. Angela nodded. Her pale hair bobbed when she did.

"I'm sorry it's been that long—"

"So, you left nearly a year ago?" My mouth was dry.

Angela looked at me with concern on her face. "Aldous... are you okay?"

"If you left nearly a year ago then she might still be there."

Could she be? But what if she weren't... what would I do then? I couldn't keep living with the Rabens. This was their house—tent—and it didn't matter they said we could stay. We had to leave soon or later. And we should have left sooner—we didn't need to stay here for nearly three months. And we were going to leave soon. We had to. We were going back to Dresden, even if Sharon wasn't there—because it was worth a shot.

CHAPTER FOURTEEN

WILL YOU BE FINE WITHOUT any money?" Ginevra asked me. I nodded.

"We'll be fine. You packed enough food to last for about a month if we save it."

Ginevra gave me a smile, one that showed the gap in between her two front teeth. I smiled back. This may be last time we saw each other.

And to think she thought I was going to murder them in their beds because I was a Nazi. Was. I was one no longer, that was clear.

Tevis and Nakita said goodbye to MSR and MAR, Kylie, Ginevra, Magnus, and Coal. Nakita had one of Kylie's old dresses and a sweater, and different shoes. Hers had been too small, and she could hardly walk in them. Tevis had a pair of old pants cut shorter and an old jacket, and his usual tattered old hat. I wasn't sure where he had picked it up.

I had my uniform jacket, with the Swastika, packed away in the bag. I couldn't wear it... it was something that made me a Nazi to everyone else. But if we were ever surrounded by other Nazis, I would have to wear it. For now, it was my save grace. I had it replaced with a dark brown jacket made of leather (Coal had gladly given it up, which I appreciated. I wonder if I had started to grow on him), and I had fixed a rip in one of my gloves, since I knew how to sew now (curtesy of Ginevra and Kylie and their undying patience).

Ginevra asked another time if we would be okay and this time I said, "*Es wird uns gut gehen.* We will be fine, don't worry. We're just going back to Dresden—it's not that far. Only... about a week on foot." That bit I tried to shimmy off as a joke, but I saw the concern flash over her face anyway.

We were going to leave while it was dark. Before we left, I turned and saw MSR and MAR salute with their arms straight out. I knew they had been fascinated a Nazi was with them. I did the same, and soon we walked far enough that the family was out of sight.

"We're really not going back," Nakita whispered in the dark, and I could tell she was trying to be brave for this. But I agreed.

"No," I whispered back to them both. "We're never going to be the same after this war. We're never going back."

It was a long time before we found more than just a dirt road. It was around six in the morning. We were exhausted from walking all night, and we stopped on the side of the road for about twenty minutes. After the twenty minutes or less had passed we kept walking. We mainly stayed on the side of the road, and we could see all the places where there had been bombs falling. Pieces of cars lay scattered across the road, and I knew it must have been because they had their headlights on; at night you were not supposed to have any lights on, and that included automobile headlights. Curbs were painted white so you could see, but it didn't do much good out where there were no curbs. Probably why those people had turned on their headlights and ended up in their graves for it.

After another hour or so, Nakita said, "I spy something brown."

Tevis looked around. "The ground? Your sweater?" The questions went on from there until I decided to guess too.

"Is it my jacket?" I said, and Nakita nodded, smiling. Tevis sighed, and I poked him. That made him give me a side smile and a shake of his head.

After a while I said, just or the fun of it, "I'm spying out of something blue."

They thought and thought. They must not have caught that I said, "am spying out of," because it took them nearly ten minutes until Tevis said, "Oh, is it your eyes? Because you're spying out of them, right?"

I told him he was right and after another couple of minutes we had gone silent again, the only sound the ground under our feet and the sound of the wind blowing, and occasionally a hawk screeching overhead.

When night fell again, we had reached a few houses. We could see that they all had a Swastika flag outside them. We kept walking, until we came to even more houses and then a tiny, still *stadtzentrum*. A town. We found a small, narrow alleyway and slept there, until we awoke from the sound of a car passing by. It startled us awake, but when we came to awareness of where we were, we were over the shock. Nakita grabbed my uniform jacket—she had been using it to sleep on—and stuffed it in the bag. Tevis grabbed his coat and threw it on, and I watched for Nazis or other German officers. When I was sure no one was going to pass us, like a Nazi or German soldier I knew, we started walking again.

CHAPTER FIFTEEN

FOR A WEEK WE WALKED.

Until, finally, we made it to Dresden.

We walked through demolished towns, roads with craters left from bombs, and hurt and dying people scattered throughout the streets. Everywhere we walked there was the word *JUDEN* on buildings, on cars. What was once a beautiful city was now as horrible as the place where I had been trained to become a soldier. A Nazi. And here was a place that was taken over by them. People walked in the streets, of course, but they did not walk slowly or make eye contact with anyone. Soldiers' cars were parked in the streets, at bars, and through the windows you could see them crowding the place. Apartment buildings were shut up with their roofs blown away, walls demolished, and windows blown out. Houses lay in ruins. People stood looking at the destruction of their homes. Piles upon piles of rubble were scattered in the street.

We came to where our neighborhood was. I felt my heart beating faster, and my throat get tighter. Nakita and Tevis were clutching my hands or my forearms. I knew from their white faces that they were taking in the destruction of our town. Our neighborhood. When we came around the corner, there was no one in sight. And most of the houses were destroyed. Then we saw it.

The house was nearly gone. Piles of bricks and other pieces of *Schutt*—rubble—lay at the base of the house. *Our house.* Or… what remained of it. Then I caught sight of someone standing at the house, looking at the word *Juden* that was painted over the only remaining wall in yellow paint. She had dark hair that was very short, she was very skinny, and she was wearing all gray, the same color as the streets and the rubble of houses. She had practically blended in. She was crossing her skinny arms. I walked closer, my eyes mainly on the house.

But then I looked closer at the woman.

My heart stopped.

I couldn't speak, and I couldn't breathe. I just stared at her, taking in what I was seeing, like if I looked away, she would disappear. Nakita and Tevis had broken away from me were at the house that someone they knew used to live in, and they didn't see her.

Then I croaked, "Sharon?"

It was loud enough, her head turned. At first her face was blank. Then her arms dropped to her sides. Her mouth fell open. We stared at each other from the twenty-foot distance. Then she said, her voice disbelieving, "Aldous?"

Tevis and Nakita heard and looked up from inspecting the damage of their friends' house, and at the same time shouted, "Mama?"

"Sharon," I whispered. Then I said, loudly, "Sharon! *Bist du das?*"

Sharon screamed, at the top of her lungs, *"Aldous!"* At this, I threw everything to the ground, and I ran. In fact, we all ran the distance between us, and when we got to her, she threw her skinny, bony arms around us, and we did the same. We stood in the street, hugging and crying, never forgetting the things we had seen and what we had endured, and never letting go of each other; Sharon, never releasing her grip on us, and looking up at me, and me kissing her hard on the lips for the first time in nearly five years; Nakita and Tevis, in between us, hugging their mama and me, and us clutching them back, and we stood there for the longest time, in the destroyed streets of Dresden. And we did this while there were others out there who had no families anymore, were stranded, and were close to their death. But not us. Sure, there was a *Krieg* on, the very middle of one. But we were also in the middle of something better.

Wir befanden uns in einen Krieg.

Wir waren in einen Familie.

A direct translation of what that means— *"We were in a war. We were in a* family."

About the Author

Naomi Reid lives with her family on their small homestead outside Topeka, Kansas. An avid reader, writer, and sketch artist, she is excited to begin her career as a published author.

www.ingramcontent.com/pod-product-compliance
Lightning Source LLC
Chambersburg PA
CBHW021335160726
47994CB00007B/2701